For K & E – *A.L.*
For Paul – *L.B.*

RED FOX

UK | USA | Canada | Ireland | Australia
India | New Zealand | South Africa

Red Fox is part of the Penguin Random House group of companies
whose addresses can be found at global.penguinrandomhouse.com.

www.penguin.co.uk
www.puffin.co.uk
www.ladybird.co.uk

Penguin
Random House
UK

First published 2016

001

Text copyright © Abie Longstaff, 2016
Illustrations copyright © Lauren Beard, 2016

The moral right of the author and illustrator has been asserted

Set in Palaino (TT) 16/23pt by Clair Lansley
Printed and bound in Great Britain by Clays Ltd, St Ives, plc

A CIP catalogue record for this book is available from the British Library

ISBN: 978–1–728–95191–9

All correspondence to:
Red Fox
Penguin Random House Children's
80 Strand, London WC2R 0RL

MIX
Paper from
responsible sources
FSC® C018179

Penguin Random house is committed to a
sustainable future for our business, our readers
and our planet. This book is made from Forest
Stewardship Council® certified paper

The Magic Potions Shop

The Blizzard Bear

Abie Longstaff & Lauren Beard

RED FOX

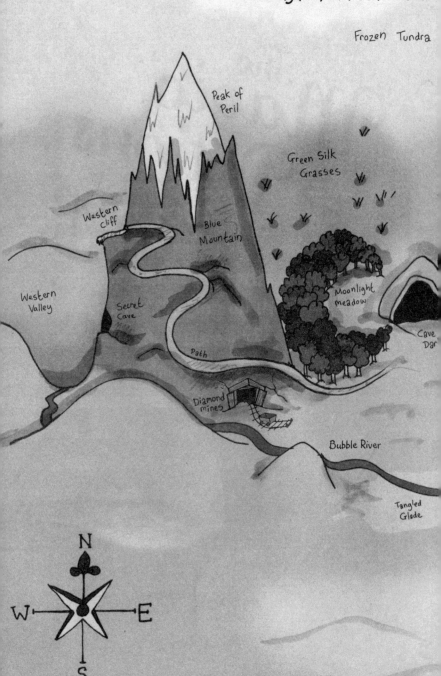

Frozen Tundra

Prince Oro's Palace

Lake Sapphire

The Potions Tree

Steadysong Forest

Troll Hills

The Vale of years

Eastern shores

Fickle Ocean

Troll Bridge

The Troll plains

Mouse Pond

Vine Curtain

Chapter One

The Kingdom of Arthwen was huge. It spread from the Frozen Tundra in the north to the Parched Desert in the south; from the Fickle Ocean in the east all the way to Western Valley.

In the middle of the kingdom, just by Lake Sapphire, was Steadysong Forest, the home of a very special tree. This tree was the largest in Arthwen. At the top was a little house with three bedrooms: one for Tibben, one for Grandpa and one for Wizz. At the base, hollowed out inside the trunk, was a very unusual shop. The shop sold potions. Creatures came here from miles around to get *Super Strength Potion* or Arm Stretch Cream or even **Never-ending Chocolate Powder**.

Grandpa was the Potions Master and he could mix any potion. He wore a cloak covered in hundreds of

Glints, the magical sign of potions skill. The Glints were all different shapes and sizes and they sparkled in the light whenever Grandpa moved.

Tibben was the Potions Apprentice. He was learning how to make potions to help all the different creatures, and to keep Harmony in the kingdom. So far he had earned two shiny Glints for his cloak. One Glint was shaped like a hexagon and the other one looked like a dark blue egg. Tibben was so proud of them! He only had three more **Glints** to go before he could take the Master's Challenge to become a Potions Master just like Grandpa. He was training every day. Not all his potions worked yet. His Cat Language Potion made him  moo all day and his **Long Beard Gel** seemed to only affect his eyebrows. Whenever he tried it, he ended up with two bushy shrubs on his face.

Wizz was helping Tibben train. She was a Gatherer – a very rare

4

and special gift –
she could find all
kinds of hidden
ingredients that
no other creature
could.

Today Tibben was
practising making Dig Fast Mix. It
was the most popular potion at this
time of year, when all the creatures
liked to hide their food and dig
their shelters for the winter. Wisgar
the Specs Mole had already made a
special trip above ground to ask for
it, and a little Star Mouse had come
in squeaking for a teeny tiny vial of
the potion.

"Right, Tibben," said Grandpa,

"I've made two lots of Dig Fast Mix. Now it's your turn."

Tibben reached under the counter and pulled out a heavy red book with golden writing. This was *The Book of Potions*, and inside were pages and pages of recipes and lists of ingredients. Tibben flicked through until he found:

Dig Fast Mix

EFFECT:
Increases digging speed by 1000 times for one hour.

INGREDIENTS:
Quick Sand
Strong Thorn

"Hmm . . . **Quick Sand** . . ." he said. "I know that's here somewhere . . ." His eyes scanned the shelves of the Potions Shop.

Wizz jumped up. "Wizz get!" she cried, and in a flash she had lifted down a bright green jar with her tail.

"Sand wooz," she said proudly. She had gathered the **Quick Sand** herself at Mouse Pond, when they went to help the River Horse.

"Thanks, Wizz." Tibben carefully sprinkled it into his **Mage Nut** training bowl. "Um . . . where's the Strong Thorn? I can never remember."

Wizz leaped up and came back with a spiky purple plant in her paws.

"You're so fast!" Tibben shook his head in amazement. He peeled off the purple bark, watching out for the spikes, and mushed it into his bowl.

Wizz peered over his shoulder. "Purple-purple weez?" she said.

"Er, yes, it is a bit purple." Tibben looked over at Grandpa, who was whistling and pretending not to notice. "Oh well, here goes . . ." He tipped the crunchy mixture into his mouth and swallowed as fast as he could.

In an instant his hands started to move.

"Yes!" he cried. "It's working!"

"Woozoo!" cried Wizz.

But Tibben's hands didn't look like they were digging. They were just jumping back and forth in tiny little movements.

"Huh?" he said.

Grandpa smiled and gave him a ball of wool. In no time flat Tibben had made a lovely warm jumper for Wizz.

"What's going on?"

Grandpa ruffled Tibben's hair. "You've made a wonderful *Speed Knit Powder* there," he said. "Can you make me a new hat?"

Tibben scowled but his hands carried on. By the end of the hour he had made:

three new jumpers . . .

six hats . . .

and a tea cosy.

He sat down, exhausted.
Grandpa and Wizz were still
laughing and dancing around in
their new hats. Tibben smiled
at them. He had to admit, the
little purple bobbles really
were works of art.

Chapter Two

Ding-dong!

The bluebell rang out and the door to the Potions Shop opened. In walked a tall elf holding a thick coat in his arms.

Tibben got up from the waiting chair. "Good morning, Albo!" he said.

"Good morning." The elf bowed. "Nice to see you again, Tibben, and you, Grandpa. And hello, little Wizz!"

"How can we help today?" asked Tibben.

"I'm travelling to the Frozen Tundra in search of Dwarfsteel," Albo answered, "and I need some kind of potion to help me see in the dark."

Grandpa stepped forward. "We have many kinds of light potion, Albo," he said, "but the Frozen Tundra will still be light at this time of year – winter is not yet here."

"I know, Potions Master," said Albo. "But on my way from Western Valley I bumped into Darnöf the Emerald Dragon. He told me that the Frozen Tundra is so dark at the

moment, even he cannot see to fly."

"Hmm," said Grandpa. "That's strange." He looked distracted as he mixed the potion. Tibben watched carefully. Grandpa could make a really strong Lightcast Potion. Whenever Tibben tried, it came out much weaker and only gave off a dim circle of light. He followed the recipe in the book as Grandpa's hands worked fast.

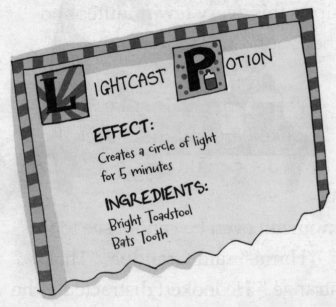

LIGHTCAST POTION

EFFECT:
Creates a circle of light for 5 minutes

INGREDIENTS:
Bright Toadstool
Bats Tooth

Grandpa squeezed the juice from the toadstool and ground up the tooth, mixing them together until he had a bowl of yellow liquid – it was

so bright Tibben had to shield his
eyes.

"Here you go," said Grandpa,
handing Albo a thin bottle. "Take a
sip of this every few minutes and
the ground will light up around
you."

"Thank you," said Albo.
He looked around the shop.
"I wonder – could I
also have one of those
lovely woollen hats?"

Tibben smiled and
handed him one from
the pile. "Good luck in the Frozen
Tundra," he said. He shivered at
the thought of it! Grandpa had
once told him that the tundra was a

dangerous place. It was cold all year round and the creatures there had to be tough and strong to survive.

"Thank you," said Albo. "Please, take some of my **Cindermoss**, straight from the Blue Mountain. I know you'll make good use of it."

"Thank-wooz!" Wizz sniffed it and patted it with her paw. Then she nodded and placed it gently in a box.

Chapter Three

Up in Tibben's room, Grandpa
and Tibben carefully opened
the *Master's Dial*. The *Dial*
measured Harmony and Blight.
When everything was peaceful and
calm, the arrow pointed up to H for
Harmony. But when something was
wrong, it moved down towards B
for Blight.

"I thought so," said Grandpa
calmly, as the arrow shifted down

to Blight. "The Frozen Tundra shouldn't be dark at this time of year."

"What's happened?" asked Tibben.

"I don't know," said Grandpa, "but whatever's gone wrong, it's our job as potions makers to fix it and bring back Harmony."

"Will you go to the Frozen Tundra?"

"Oh no." Grandpa shook his head. "I'm too old and tired to make that kind of journey."

Tibben looked down. Grandpa was nearly a hundred years old. It would soon be time for him to retire to the Vale of Years. Then it would be Tibben's turn to be the Potions Master. Tibben frowned. He didn't like to think about that.

"Tibben" – Grandpa took his hand – "you need to go to the Frozen Tundra and find out what is causing the Blight."

Tibben took a deep breath.

Grandpa patted his hand. "You and Wizz are a good team," he said. "Together you can bring back Harmony, I know you can."

Tibben nodded bravely. It would be good to have Wizz with him – she always made him feel better.

"Now, why don't you start packing," said Grandpa. "I'll go downstairs and make you some potions for the journey."

"OK," said Tibben, but when Grandpa had gone, his heart started pounding and he began to shake. He sat down on his bed. The Frozen Tundra! He remembered Grandpa's stories about the icy land up there. It was filled with scary-sounding

creatures like Frost Wolves and Blizzard Bears and, high in the air, enormous Shadow Owls swooped across the snowy plains. Tibben pulled out the map from the drawer beside his bed and stared at the wide expanse of snow and ice. The Frozen Tundra was such a long way north! He had never been that far from home.

Suddenly his bedroom door flew open.

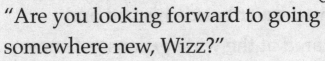

"Woooooozoooooo!"
Wizz came bouncing
in. She was so
excited she could
hardly keep still.

Tibben couldn't
help laughing at her.
"Are you looking forward to going
somewhere new, Wizz?"

"Wooz! Wooz!" She held out
her paws and Tibben could see
her Gathering Diary. "Wizz get
plants," she explained.

Wizz loved finding new plants.
She had filled her diary with
sketches and scribbles about all
the different varieties she had
found, and there were pages with

drawings and bits of twig and leaf
that meant nothing to Tibben, but
were very precious to Wizz.

All at once Tibben felt better.
Wizz was right – it would be an
adventure! They would get to see

all sorts of plants and creatures, and a whole new area of Arthwen.

"Let's get packing!" he cried, and Wizz whizzed around the room, pulling open Tibben's drawers to find his jumpers and socks.

By the time they got back downstairs, Grandpa had made them a big pile of bottles and jars. There was **Warming Liquid**, made from the **Cindermoss** Albo had brought. There was Lightcast Potion, to help them see. There was even *Sticking Potion* to stick their new woollen hats firmly to their heads.

30

Tibben grabbed a jar of
Dig Fast Mix, just in case they
needed to dig a snow shelter,
and filled his pockets with
handfuls of ingredients so he could
make his own potions. Then he tied
his **Mage Nut** bowl to his backpack
and opened the door of the Potions
Shop.

Grandpa hugged them both.
"Good luck," he said, "and stay
warm!"

Chapter Four

Tibben and Wizz walked due north from the Potions Tree, passing all the way through Steadysong Forest. As they walked, Wizz picked Strong Thorn for making more Dig Fast Mix, and some fresh Gumspider Web for climbing and sticking potions. Every time she found a plant, she squeaked with excitement and wrote its location down in her diary. She seemed to sniff out plants in all

kinds of hidden places. Outside
Prince Oro's palace she even
managed to find the very rare
Glass Flower, a see-through
plant used for making **Handsome
Cream**.

"Wow!" said Tibben. "Well done,
Wizz!" He looked up at the grand
palace towering above them. It was
so smart and elegant, he suddenly
felt shabby in his old cloak. He
peered through the fancy gates,
hoping to catch a glimpse of the
famous Prince Oro!

"Come-come weez!" Wizz called.

Tibben turned round – Wizz was
right; there was no time to spare.
He took one last look through the

gates and hurried to catch up
with her.

On they went, further and
further north. The air was getting
colder and Tibben was glad he had
knitted the extra jumpers. It was
also getting darker. He checked
his map – they were nearly at the
Frozen Tundra! He felt in his bag
for Grandpa's *Lightcast Potion* and
took a little sip. All at once a circle
of light appeared
on the ground
and everything
inside the circle
shone brightly.
Wherever
Tibben

walked, the light moved with him, and Wizz had great fun jumping in and out of the circle.

"You're making me dizzy!" Tibben laughed. Wizz giggled and jumped out of the circle again to pick some *Vary Violet*, used for Shrinking Potion.

Soon the ground underfoot became crunchy with frost, and as they walked into the Frozen Tundra, the snow fell more thickly. Tibben pulled his hat down over his ears and felt in his backpack for the *Sticking Potion* to keep it there. But just as he was searching, he heard a *smash!* There was a flash

37

of light and Tibben looked down.

"Oh no!" he cried – he had dropped the bottle of *Lightcast Potion*!

"Weeeeez!" cried Wizz.

"I know!" said Tibben. "I'm so sorry, Wizz." They watched in despair as the light potion trickled away into the snow.

"I'll make some more." Tibben took out his **Mage Nut** bowl and opened *The Book of Potions*. The circle of light around him was growing dim – the potion inside him was wearing off! Soon it would be dark again; too dark to see. Frantically Tibben tried to remember exactly what Grandpa had done. He squeezed the *Bright Toadstool* as quickly as he could. The light seemed to be fading faster and faster now. He ground the **Bat's Tooth** and added the powder, stirring until the last bit of light disappeared.

In the blackness Tibben felt around for the bowl. He lifted it to his lips and took a sip. A circle of dim light appeared, much softer and duskier than before.

Tibben's potion was nowhere near as powerful as Grandpa's.

"Sorry, Wizz," he said again.

She climbed up to put her arms around his neck.

"No worry wooz," she said, and Tibben smiled.

Without Grandpa's extra-strong potion, he had to walk much more

carefully. He shuffled through the snow, his toes growing colder with every step. Tibben shivered and pulled his cloak tight around him. *I'm a pretty rubbish Potions Apprentice,* he thought to himself. *Not only did I drop Grandpa's potion but I can't even make a proper one of my own.*

"Look-a-wooz!" cried Wizz all of a sudden. Tibben couldn't see anything in the darkness, but Wizz had jumped out of his arms and was sniffing at the ice.

"What is it?" he asked.

"Shine-weez," said Wizz.

Tibben looked closely. Was something shining underneath the ice? He wasn't sure; but Wizz was. Tibben put down his bag and felt around for the jar of **Warming**

Liquid Grandpa had made. He
carefully poured a tiny bit onto the
ice. It melted instantly to form a
small pool of water. Wizz put her
paw into the icy liquid and pulled
out a strange see-through object.
Tibben had never seen
anything like it before.
It had jagged edges
made of thousands
of tiny shards of
glass.

At least, Tibben
thought it was glass.

Wizz turned the object over in her
paws and sniffed it. She shrugged
her shoulders and looked at Tibben.
"Funny glass-a-wooz," she said.

"Yes, it *is* funny glass." Tibben took it from Wizz. "Hmm . . ."

He screwed up his face. The glass was giving him a strange feeling; a feeling of warmth and strength. Tibben shook his head – his mind must be playing tricks on him!

He put the glass into his bag. Then he had another sip of his weak Lightcast Potion. But this time, to his amazement, his circle of light shone as brightly as Grandpa's had! Tibben looked at Wizz in wonder. "My potion is working!" he cried.

Wizz smiled at him.

Tibben shook his head in amazement. He had no idea why his potion was suddenly so powerful but he felt wonderful – like he could do anything or make any potion!

Tibben laughed and took Wizz's paw. Together they set off across the ice.

Chapter Five

Tibben's *Lightcast Potion* was so strong now that they could easily see where they were going. They slid over the ice, laughing and jumping over mounds of snow. Ahead of them was an enormous snow hill. Tibben ran at it as fast as he could, and rolled down the other side, whooping and cheering.

Wizz followed, rolling so fast she was just a blur of white fur against white snow. "Woozoooooooo!"

They stood up and brushed themselves down. Tibben lifted his head to hear a *tap-tap-tapping* sound. Just near where they had landed stood an Ice Dwarf digging with his pick. He was small and round, with a shiny metal belt and a long black beard tied in a plait.

"Hello!" called Tibben.

"Oh!" said the Ice Dwarf. "It's the Potions Master!" He bowed.

"Actually," said Tibben, "that's Grandpa. I'm Tibben, the Potions Apprentice – but I do have two Glints. Look!" He showed the dwarf his cloak. "I'm here to find out about the darkness."

"Thank goodness. We are all so worried. I'm Delvïg." The Ice Dwarf held out his hand. "I hope you can help us, Tibben. Finding Dwarfsteel is hard enough, but now we can hardly see a thing. I'm exhausted from digging in the dark." He stretched. "My back is aching and I've only found a small pile." Delvïg pointed to a mound of white metal.

"Would you like some Dig Fast Mix?" Tibben offered him the bottle.

"Thank you," said Delvïg. "That's really going to help. Please take a piece of Dwarfsteel in return."

Tibben took the metal and put

it into his backpack.

In the distance they heard a strange *thump*, then a rumble.

"What's that?" asked Tibben.

"I don't know." The dwarf scratched his head. "I've heard it on and off since the sky went dark."

"Hmm," said Tibben. "I think we should head towards that sound, Wizz."

"Wooz." She nodded.

"Thank you, Delvïg."

"Stay warm," he answered, tipping his mining helmet.

Tibben and Wizz went on towards the noise. With every step they took, it seemed as if the

thumping was growing louder.
And with every thump the earth
shook and rumbled.

Soon they came to a yellow Snow
Sprite standing under a tree. She
had long silky hair and pointy ears.
In her tiny fingers she held a candle.

Her silver wings fluttered when
she saw Tibben. "Oh, Potions
Apprentice!" she said. "Thank
goodness you are here. My icicle
sculptures won't stick to the trees.
All this thumping is making them
fall off."

Tibben handed her some
Sticking Potion. "This should
help," he said.

"Thank you." In return the sprite

gave Tibben a strand of her beautiful *Snow Hair.* "My name is Eira," she said. She looked up at him with huge eyes. "Will you fix the darkness? We're all so frightened. The little animals won't even come out of their ice holes and none of us can get any work done."

"I'm going to try my best," said Tibben.

"Thank you," said Eira. "Stay warm." She waved as they walked on.

Tibben waved back, trying to look confident. He hoped and hoped he could help.

Chapter Six

The Frozen Tundra was in complete
darkness. The only light was in the
circle Tibben had made – everything
else was pitch black. It was an
eerie feeling, walking on into the
blackness. It was so cold and the
only noise came from the crunching
of their feet on the ice, and the
mysterious thumping that was
growing louder and louder. There
was a strange mist in the air and

the land felt empty and desolate.

"I don't like this," said Tibben, his voice echoing across the snowy plains: . . . *like this* . . . *like this* . . . *like this* . . .

"No weez." Wizz nodded. "Dark, dark."

"And we haven't seen a single creature for ages." There were no Snee Hares hopping through the snow, and no Shadow Owls swooping overhead. There weren't even any Blizzard Bears; although secretly, Tibben was rather relieved about this.

"The darkness seems to be scaring everyone away," he said. "Something is very wrong. Oh, Wizz, I hope I can fix it."

"Wooz," said Wizz, and she
put her paw in Tibben's hand.
They walked on, hand in paw,
until . . .

"Stop wooz!" Wizz squeaked
loudly. She stopped dead and
Tibben almost ran into the back
of her.

"What is it?" he asked.

Wizz pointed ahead and, at the
edge of the circle of light, Tibben

saw a hole in the ice. The thumping noise seemed to be coming from deep inside the hole. Tibben also saw tiny sparks of light shooting up into the air.

He inched forward nervously till he was standing at the very edge of

the hole. He peered down, and there, at the bottom, was a young Blizzard Bear.

Tibben gulped. Although he had heard about them, he had never actually seen a Blizzard Bear in real life before. This one was pale blue, with big teeth and spiky-looking fur. He was very angry; he was standing up on his hind legs, and bashing the walls of the hole with one of his huge front paws. Every time he did so, he sent out tiny sparks, and the thumping noise echoed across the Frozen Tundra. Tibben looked at Wizz nervously. The bear didn't seem very friendly and Tibben couldn't stop staring at his enormous claws.

He took a deep
breath. "Hello!"
he called down
into the hole.

The Blizzard
Bear looked up. His eyes
were narrow and cross. Hot breath
came out of his snout and rose up
out of the hole.

He growled at Tibben.

"Um . . ." stuttered Tibben.
"Er . . . do you need some help?
I'm . . . um . . . Tibben, the
Potions Apprentice."

The Blizzard Bear huffed and
turned away. He began to thump
the wall with his paw again.

"OK," said Tibben. He needed the bear to calm down. "Please stop that."

"Weez?" Wizz asked Tibben.

"I think he's trying to do a Frost Crash, Wizz."

Wizz looked puzzled.

"It's what bears do to bash into mountains and make caves," Tibben explained. "It makes a big explosion."

Wizz peered down into the hole. "No-big wooz," she said, shaking her head.

"No," agreed Tibben. "I think he's having trouble."

The Blizzard Bear looked up. "You talking about me?" He snarled out another hot breath, then struck the ground again and again with his heavy paw, causing another flurry of sparks to fly up. "It's not fair!" he cried. "All the big bears can do a proper Frost Crash. Mine just makes little sparks!" He reared up on his hind legs once more and yelled, "I want to get out of this hole!"

"Maybe we can help," Tibben said calmly. "What's your name?"

"I'm Karhu," the bear growled in reply.

"How did you get into this hole, Karhu?"

"I fell. I was trying—" Karhu suddenly stopped. For the first time he looked a bit embarrassed. His blue fur turned pink as he spoke. "I was trying to catch the Ice Star," he admitted.

Tibben gasped. Stars weren't for catching! Especially not the Ice Star. The Ice Star was magical; its light brought warmth and Harmony to the kingdom.

Karhu saw how shocked Tibben was and he began to explain himself, but his growly voice sounded like it was full of tears.

"Dad says it's really powerful. And I thought" – he sniffed – "I thought it might help me make a

proper *Frost Crash*. So I found a rock."
Tibben raised his eyebrows. He
waited to hear what the bear would say.

"I climbed up there." Karhu pointed,
and Tibben peered into the darkness.
He could just make out the shadow
of an enormous hill. "It's the highest
mountain in the Frozen Tundra,"
said Karhu. "I threw my rock
as hard as I could . . .

It hit the star and I saw it wobble."

Tibben gave Wizz a worried look.

"The star shot down from the sky. I don't know where it is now. When it hit the ground the star went dark and all its sparkle disappeared."

Well, of course it did, thought Tibben. *The Ice Star should be in the sky. It can't shine on the ground.*

"Then everything else went dark

and I couldn't see," the bear went on. "I stumbled down the mountain and fell into this hole." He gave a little sob.

Tibben sat back on his heels. He felt very cross. That naughty little bear had plunged the whole of the Frozen Tundra into darkness! He could feel himself getting

angrier and angrier, and as he did
so the dark seemed darker and
the cold seemed colder. Tibben
shivered. The air was heavy and
misty, and all he wanted to do was
give up and go home. Why should
he help this bad bear? He should
just leave him there!

"Help weez?" squeaked Wizz.
Tibben looked at her and folded
his arms, but Wizz curled her tail
around his wrist and tugged. He
looked at her. Then back at the bear.

"No weeeeez," said Wizz.
"Help," she said again.

Tibben sighed. Wizz was right. He *had* to help the bear. That was his job. Even if the darkness was Karhu's fault, Tibben couldn't leave him in the hole.

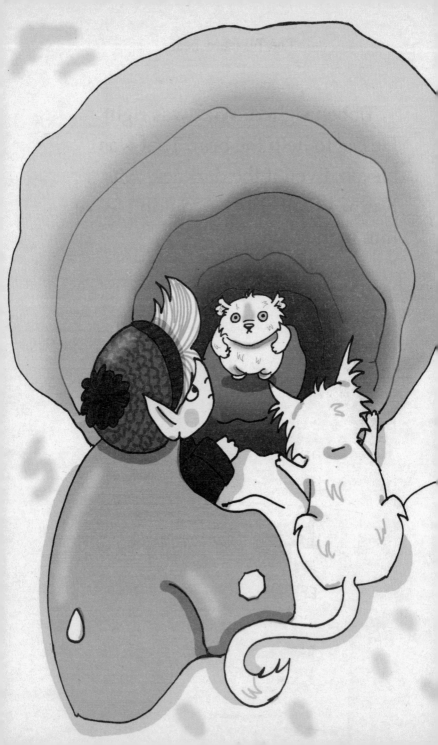

Chapter Seven

Tibben leaned over the hole. "I'm going to get you out," he called down. "I just have to work out how." He opened *The Book of Potions* and turned the pages until he found:

MAGIC ROPE

EFFECT:
Creates a solid levitating rope

INGREDIENTS:
Dwarf Steel
Snow Hair

Tibben had the **Dwarfsteel** from Delvïg and the *Snow Hair* from Eira. He got the ingredients out of his bag. But how could he mix them together? The **Dwarfsteel** was just a lump of white metal and the *Snow Hair* was a thin strand of silver.

Tibben put the **Dwarfsteel** into his **Mage Nut** bowl. He tried to imagine what *Magic Rope* might look like. It was a difficult task. He was still feeling cross and a sense of emptiness was creeping over him. Tibben knew this feeling; he had felt it before – in the cave where he found Wizz, and in the Tangled Glade when the River Horse was sad. It was Blight; a feeling of

sadness and fear and emptiness,
when it feels like nothing can go
right and everything seems wrong.
Tibben took a breath. He had to
fight it.

Then he felt Wizz's paw touch
his hand. Tibben smiled. If he made
this potion right, maybe he'd even
get a **Glint**! All at once he felt much
better. He was determined to give
Magic Rope a try.

Tibben bent
over the bowl
and wrapped
the silver
strand
around
the

white metal. He took his spoon and stirred it once, then again.

Before his eyes, the *Snow Hair* twisted more and more tightly around the metal. It shook and started to grow. Up and up out of the bowl it rose, until it became a hard silver rope floating upright in the air. He had done it! He had actually managed to make *Magic Rope*!

Tibben looked down at his cloak. Surely he had earned a **Glint**? But no . . . He shook his head.

"Dark weez," said Wizz and pointed up.

Tibben nodded. Wizz was

right. He wouldn't get a **Glint** until he had brought Harmony back, and to do that he needed to put an end to the darkness.

Tibben lifted the *Magic Rope* and dropped it into the ice hole. The rope hovered in the air, hard and strong.

"Climb up," he said, but Karhu shook his head. For a moment he looked really small and frightened; just a bundle of blue fluff.

"It's all right," Tibben told him. "The rope will hold – it's *Magic Rope*." But Karhu shrank back into a corner.

"Here, I'll show you." Tibben held onto the rope and slid right down to the bottom of the hole. The Blizzard Bear's eyes widened in amazement.

"Now you try," said Tibben. "Don't worry, I'll be here to catch you."

Karhu looked at the rope nervously. He put out one shaky paw

78

and clasped it to his fluffy tummy.

"That's it," said Tibben. "Now, one paw over the other . . ."

Karhu did as Tibben told him, and in no time he had climbed all the way out of the hole. Tibben followed him up and stepped onto the cold snowy ground.

Chapter Eight

"Thank you, thank you," said Karhu. "I'm sorry I was cross. I was so scared. And I'm sorry I took the star. I wish I hadn't."

Tibben gave him a hug and stroked his soft fur. All of a sudden everything felt better. Although it was still dark, the air was somehow brighter and cleaner.

"We're going to find the Ice Star and put it back," he told the bear.

"I'll help," offered Karhu.

"Wizz help," said Wizz.

"Thank you," said Tibben.
"Now, Karhu, what did the star
look like?"

"Well" – Karhu wrinkled up his
furry face – "it was a strange shape
– all bumpy around the edges –
and it was see-through. A bit like
lots of pieces of glass."

Tibben gasped, remembering
what Wizz had found under the
ice.

She jumped up and down in
excitement. "Wizz find! Wizz find!
Funny glass!" she cried.

"Yes," said Tibben. "Wizz found
something just like that." He

opened his bag and
held out the jagged
glassy object. "Is this
the Ice Star?" he asked.

"Yes!" Karhu grinned a wide
toothy grin.

"But it's tiny," said Tibben.

The bear shrugged. "It was
bigger before," he said.

"It belongs in the sky," said
Tibben. "It must have shrunk when
it landed on the earth, and lost
its light."

He turned the star over and over
in his hands. It really was a strange
object. The longer he held it, the
more Tibben sensed its warmth
and power.

All at once he realized something. It was the Ice Star that had made all his potions work! That was why he had managed to make *Magic Rope*, and why his *Lightcast Potion* was just as strong as Grandpa's – because he was carrying the star! But now he'd have to give it up.

He thought about the hard work he had to put into making his potions, and how often they'd gone wrong or been too weak. The Ice Star could fix all that. For a moment Tibben understood why Karhu had wanted the star. It was so powerful! With the star, all his potions would work and he'd get all the **Glints** he wanted!

Tibben looked up into the
darkness. He remembered how
Delvïg's back hurt from digging
in the dark, and what Eira had
said about the little animals being
scared.

"Star wooz?" asked Wizz. She tapped his arm.

Tibben looked down into her big blue eyes. She was staring up at him, waiting for him to make the right decision. He looked at the star in his hands. He knew what to do. Using the star would be cheating. How would he ever become a real Potions Master if he couldn't make his own potions without help?

"We have to get the Ice Star back into the sky," he said, and he opened *The Book of Potions*. He thumbed through the pages, looking for the right potion. "There!" he cried, and pointed to:

Shooting Star Remedy

EFFECT:
Restores a fallen star into the sky

INGREDIENTS:
Cindermoss
Shatter Petals
Exploding Powder

"We've already got **Cindermoss**, thanks to Albo," said Tibben. "What about **Shatter Petals**? Can you find those, Wizz?"

Wizz closed her eyes. She put a paw in the air, scrunched up her nose and sniffed. Then she opened her eyes with a snap and headed off to the left. Tibben followed to give her some light.

Wizz brushed the snow aside with her tail. All Tibben could see was white. There were no plants or flowers anywhere. But Wizz kept brushing and brushing. The snow made a big pile to the side, and still she brushed.

All at once she cried out and her paw shot into the snow. When she pulled it back, she was clutching a stripy blue flower.

"Is that it?" asked Tibben.

"Wooz." Wizz nodded. She took out her diary to draw the plant and write down where it was found.

"Well done!" said Tibben. He

looked at the recipe again. "Now we need *Exploding Powder*. I'll have to make that."

But when Tibben looked up the recipe, he realized there was a problem. He had no *Jumping Flint,* no **Five Seeds** and no **Red-Hot Orchid**.

"Can you find any of these, Wizz?" he asked.

She shook her head. "Wizz no find in cold cold." She opened her **Gathering Diary** and showed Tibben.

He looked at her drawings and saw what she meant – none of the ingredients came from the Frozen Tundra. *Jumping Flint* came

from the Blue Mountain,
Five Seeds were found in the
Parched Desert and **Red-Hot
Orchid** grew in Steadysong Forest.
Wizz couldn't gather any of the
ingredients here!

"What shall we do?" wondered Tibben. "We'll never get the star back now."

He stared down gloomily. Then, out of the corner of his eye, he saw Karhu. The Blizzard Bear was still practising his Frost Crash. Little

sparks were flying out as he struck the ground with his paws.

"Wait a minute!" cried Tibben. Frost Crash was a kind of explosion, wasn't it?

"Karhu!" he called. "Please can you try your Frost Crash again? Come over here by the Ice Star. It will make your crash much more powerful, and I think . . . I think . . . we can use it to put the star back into the sky."

Chapter Nine

Tibben put the Ice Star down in his bowl. He scattered **Shatter Petals** until the star was covered with tiny bits of blue and white stripes. Then he added the **Cindermoss**.

"OK," he said. "It's your turn, Karhu. Please could you do your **Frost Crash**, and I'll stir the mixture."

Karhu stood on his back legs, lifting his mighty paws high in the

air. Then he brought them down fast
and hard. He hit the ground with
a massive

Crash!

Now that he was near the star, the crash was much louder and more powerful than before! The ground shook and rumbled, and sparks flew into the air.

Tibben stirred the star round and round in his **Mage Nut** bowl. It started to glow. "I think it's working!" he cried. "Do it again, Karhu!"

The bear struck the ground again and again, and with every crash the star grew bigger and brighter. Soon it was so bright that Tibben had to shield his eyes.

"That's it!" he cried. The star was growing fast now and he could feel heat coming from the centre of the bowl. The Ice Star started to shudder, and it was all Tibben could do to keep his **Mage Nut** bowl steady. He gripped the edges tight while the star rocked crazily.

"Watch out!" he yelled as
it started to rise out of the
bowl. There was a flash
of bright white light,
and then  **Whooooosh!**

The star shot out of the bowl
and up into the dark sky. The three

friends watched it fly higher and higher, until suddenly it stopped and settled into place. Instantly the sky lit up and the darkness was gone!

Tibben could see the Frozen Tundra clearly for the first time. He gasped – it was so much more beautiful than he had realized! The ice sparkled and there were white *Frostpine* trees lining the horizon. Tibben smiled. Even though the land was cold, he felt a warm glow inside. He had stopped the Blight! The air was fresh and everything was right.

Tibben jumped as he caught sight of a dark shape on the white snow. He looked up to see an enormous Shadow Owl flying by. The owl

tipped his wings and hooted his thanks to Tibben. One by one, creatures came out of their ice holes, happy to be able to see. Snee Hares bounded across the ice and Pearly Squirrels chattered in gratitude.

Tibben smiled to see everyone enjoying the light.

"Thank you, Tibben."
Karhu bowed low,
his black nose
touching the
ice. "I'm
sorry I was
rude to you
and I promise

I will never disturb a star again."

Tibben gave him a hug. "Thank
you for your help, Karhu. Your
Frost Crash was wonderful. Keep
practising, and one day you'll be
able to do it without the Ice Star."

"Stay warm," Karhu answered,
raising a paw in thanks.

Everyone clapped and stamped
and whistled and cheered.

"Wooz!" cried Wizz all of a sudden. She pointed to Tibben's cloak. It was a Glint! He could see it shining next to the other two.

This was *Pearl* level – the **Glint** was round and creamy white, with sparkles at its edges. Tibben grinned at Wizz.

"Grandpa wooz," she said.

"Yes," said Tibben. "Let's go home."

Chapter Ten

On the way home they met all kinds
of creatures. Shiver Fawns stamped
their hooves in greeting and baby
Snee Hares flashed their white tails.

Ahead, Eira the Snow Sprite
stood with all her relatives, smiling
and waving, and Delvïg saluted
them with his pick.

"Thank you, Tibben," he called,
pointing to an enormous pile of
Dwarfsteel.

It wasn't long before the snow started to melt at their feet and they were leaving the Frozen Tundra.

"Goodbye!" Tibben waved.

"Stay warm!" the creatures called back.

Then, hand in paw, Tibben and Wizz ran past Prince Oro's palace and all the way through Steadysong Forest, right to the largest tree in the kingdom.

At the door of the Potions Shop Grandpa was waiting.

"Hooray!" he cried when he saw them.

"Grandpa! Grandpa!" Tibben cried. "I've got another **Glint!**"

He and Wizz told Grandpa all about their adventure.

"I had to

help the Blizzard Bear, even though it was all his fault," explained Tibben.

"You did the right thing, Tibben," Grandpa replied. "All creatures need our help, even the ones who have made mistakes."

Tibben nodded.

Wizz opened her Gathering Diary to show Grandpa. He spent ages looking at the new plants and seeds she had found – Vary Violet, Shatter Petals and Glass Flower. They talked about every bit of bark and petal for so long that Tibben began to yawn.

"I'll make some Hazelwood tea, shall I?" he said, but Grandpa was

so interested in the diary he didn't even look up. Tibben shrugged and put the little pot on the stove. He rubbed the edge of his new **Glint** and listened to its low hum. Three **Glints**! He smiled to himself. Only two to go, and then he could take the Master's Challenge! Then he'd be a Potions Master!

Tibben looked around the
Potions Shop at all the wonderful
ingredients waiting for him. In
the background he could hear
Wizz chattering to Grandpa,
and Grandpa's low steady voice
answering her. He rubbed his cold
hands together over the steam from
the pot. It was good to be home!

Potions

Extracts from *The Book of Potions:*

Arm Stretch Cream
Effect: Lengthens arms
Ingredients:
- Stretch Thistle
- Fast Lotus

Cat Language Potion
Effect: Allows the drinker to speak to and understand cats
Ingredients:
- Sky Whisker
- Yowl Seed
- Thunder Rumble

Dig Fast Mix
Effect: Increases digging speed by 1,000 times for one hour
Ingredients:
- Quick Sand
- Strong Thorn

Exploding Powder
Effect: Causes any substance to explode
Ingredients:
- Jumping Flint
- Fire Seeds
- Red-Hot Orchid

Handsome Cream
Effect: Makes the drinker 100 times more attractive
Ingredients:
- Glass Flower
- Chrysalis Powder
- Lily of Loveliness

Lightcast Potion
Effect: Creates a circle of light for five minutes
Ingredients:
- Bright Toadstool
- Bat's Tooth

Long Beard Gel
Effect: Gives drinker a super long beard
Ingredients:
- Unicorn Whisker
- Stretch Thistle

Magic Rope
Effect: Creates a solid levitating rope
Ingredients:
- Dwarfsteel
- Snow Hair

Never-ending Chocolate Powder
Effect: Creates refilling pile of chocolates
Ingredients:
- Sugar Strand
- Unicorn Whisker

Shooting Star Remedy
Effect: Restores a fallen star into the sky
Ingredients:
- Cindermoss
- Shatter Petals
- Exploding Powder

Shrinking Potion

Effect: Makes the drinker shrink in size for 10 minutes
Ingredients:
- Vary Violet
- Mouse Water
- Low Root

Speed Knit Powder

Effect: Makes drinker's hands knit for one hour
Ingredients:
- Quick Sand
- Strong Thorn

Sticking Potion

Effect: Sticks anything to anything
Ingredients:
- Gumspider Web
- Red Clay
- Troll Slime

Super Strength Potion

Effect: Gives the drinker super strength for one hour
Ingredients:
- Sturdy Vine
- Fire Seeds

Warming Liquid

Effect: Increases warmth by 28 degrees for five seconds
Ingredients:
- Fire Seeds
- Cindermoss

Ingredients

Extracts from
The Glossary of Magic Ingredients

Bat's Tooth
Exchange with the bats of Troll Hills for **Super Hearing Gel.** Used in **Light Potions, Seeing Potions** and **Fortune Teller Cream**

Bright Toadstool
Grows in Moonlight Meadow, among the pixies. Used in **Light Potions** and **Dress-Up Potion**

Cindermoss
Grown by elves on the Blue Mountain. Used in **Warming Potions** and **Shooting Star Remedy**

Fire Seeds
Pick these from the Burning Flower in the Parched Desert. Used for **Fire Dance Potion, Warming Liquid** and **Exploding Powder**

Frost Crash
Request from the Blizzard Bears in the Frozen Tundra

Glass Flower
Rare ingredient found in palaces. Used in **Beauty Potion, Handsome Cream** and **Transformation Gel**

Gumspider Web
Found in Steadysong Forest. Take one strand at a time only. Used for **Sticking Potion, Climbing Potion** and **Tidy Thread**

Jumping Flint
Found in the Diamond Mines under the Blue Mountain. Silver stone. Used in Fire Dance Potion, **Mop Dance Gel** and **Exploding Powder.** Beware – this stone will leap about once cut

Quick Sand
Covers the ground at Mouse Pond. Beware. Used in all **Speed Potions** and **Ten Legs Potion**

Red Clay
Found at the bottom of Lake Sapphire and Bubble River. Used for **Sticking Potion**

Red-Hot Orchid
Grows in Steadysong Forest. Do not touch the leaves. Used in **Fire Dance Potion**, **Exploding Powder** and for making **Magic Coal**

Shatter Petals
From a stripy blue flower picked in the Frozen Tundra. Used for **Shooting Star Remedy**

Sky Whisker
Exchange with Sky Cats of the Blue Mountain for Essence of Milk. Used for **Pouncing Potion** and **Language Potions**

Snow Hair
Exchange with Snow Sprites in the Frozen Tundra. Used for **Magic Rope**

Stretch Thistle
Grows in the Green Silk Grasses. Tall spiky green plant. Used for **Growth Potions**, **High Reach Potion**, **Arm Stretch Cream** and **Ten Legs Potion**

Strong Thorn
Pick very carefully in Steadysong Forest. Look for purple spikes. Used in **Piercing and Cutting Potions** as well as **Speed Knit Powder**

Sturdy Vine
Found in the Tangled Glade. Used for all **Strength Potions**

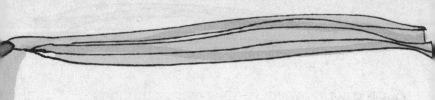

Sugar Strand
Exchange with Sugar Bees in the Green Silk Grasses for
Super Speeding Potion. Used for **Kindness Potion** and
Dessert Potions

Troll Slime
Grows under bridges in Troll Hills. Used for **Sticking Potion**,
Climbing Potion and **Tidy Thread**

Unicorn Whisker
Exchange with Twilight Unicorns on Moonlight Meadow for
Diamond Powder. Used in all **Speed Potions**, **Hair Potions**
and **Regeneration Potions**

Vary Violet
Found in the Frozen Tundra. Used for **Change Potions**

Yowl Seed
Furry Yowl Plant grows in the Green Silk Grasses. Distinctive
orange and black stripy fur. Used for **Language Potions** and
Monster Fur Cream

Wizz's Quiz

Test your knowledge – how many questions can you answer?

1) Which potion will help you to see in the dark?

2) Which two ingredients do you need to make *Dig Fast Mix*?

3) What does Tibben create after he drinks *Dig Fast Mix*?

4) What does Wizz find outside Prince Oro's Palace?

5) Which potion does Tibben use to help the Blizzard Bear out of the hole?

6) From whom does Tibben get *Snow Hair*?

7) What does the Blizzard Bear do to help put the Ice Star back in the sky?

8) What colour is the Blizzard Bear's fur?

Turn to the back of the book for the solution to this puzzle!

A Frosty Wordsearch

It's getting pretty chilly! There are ten frosty words hidden in this word search that you might encounter in the Frozen Tundra – can you find them?

D	F	G	H	J	D	W	S	N	A	E	G	P	S	Z
W	O	E	C	I	P	W	R	H	N	C	A	F	G	H
I	E	B	A	E	E	L	S	Q	T	R	A	T	S	B
T	B	M	N	F	B	X	W	O	S	A	S	F	B	Q
S	O	L	H	Z	E	E	D	C	I	M	N	S	S	B
C	G	M	I	S	T	D	B	F	L	E	I	N	I	O
L	B	C	D	Z	R	R	E	P	Z	N	X	O	U	L
Z	U	T	I	F	Z	X	S	F	Z	I	I	W	L	T
F	B	H	R	E	E	A	N	L	G	P	O	F	T	D
L	O	A	E	A	B	S	R	C	D	T	A	E	W	E
O	W	R	T	E	A	T	E	D	S	S	C	L	J	F
D	S	Z	Z	L	F	E	P	A	O	O	R	H	P	F
L	O	F	T	D	B	E	I	R	K	R	O	S	I	L
I	S	N	O	W	F	L	A	K	E	F	E	D	R	A
F	G	B	I	R	R	D	O	F	W	P	R	E	R	K

ice ✓   snowflake
snow ✓   dwarf
blizzard ✓   star ✓
steel   dark
frostpine   mist ✓

Turn to the back of the book for the solution to this puzzle!

Snow Scramble

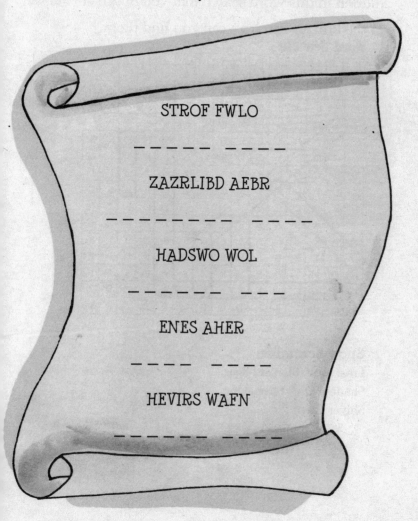

The creatures below have got themselves
muddled in the snow. Can you unscramble them?

STROF FWLO

_ _ _ _ _   _ _ _ _

ZAZRLIBD AEBR

_ _ _ _ _ _ _ _   _ _ _ _

HADSWO WOL

_ _ _ _ _ _   _ _ _

ENES AHER

_ _ _ _   _ _ _ _

HEVIRS WAFN

_ _ _ _ _ _   _ _ _ _

Turn to the back of the book for the solution to this puzzle!

Solutions

Wizz's Quiz:

Lightcast Potion; Quick Sand and Strong Thorn;
Three jumpers, six hats, and a tea cosy; A Glass Flower;
Magic Rope; The Snow Sprite; A Frost Crash; Blue

Word Search:

D	F	G	H	J	D	W	S	N	A	E	G	P	S	Z
W	O	E	C	I	P	W	R	H	N	C	A	F	G	H
I	E	B	A	E	E	L	S	Q	T	R	A	T	S	B
T	B	M	N	F	B	X	W	O	S	A	S	F	B	Q
S	O	L	H	Z	E	E	D	C	I	M	N	S	S	B
C	G	M	I	S	T	D	B	F	L	E	I	N	I	O
L	B	C	D	Z	R	R	E	P	Z	N	X	O	U	L
Z	U	T	I	F	Z	X	S	F	Z	I	I	W	L	T
F	B	H	R	E	E	A	N	L	G	P	O	F	T	D
L	Q	A	E	A	B	S	R	C	D	T	A	E	W	E
O	W	R	T	E	A	T	E	D	S	S	C	L	J	F
D	S	Z	Z	L	F	E	P	A	O	O	R	H	P	F
L	O	F	T	D	B	E	I	R	K	R	O	S	I	L
I	S	N	O	W	F	L	A	K	E	F	E	D	R	A
F	G	B	I	R	R	D	O	F	W	P	R	E	R	K

Snow Scramble:

Frost Wolf; Blizzard Bear;
Shadow Owl; Snee Hare;
Shiver Fawn